First published in the United Kingdom by
HarperCollins *Children's Books* in 2024
HarperCollins *Children's Books* is a division of HarperCollins*Publishers* Ltd
1 London Bridge Street
London SE1 9GF

www.harpercollins.co.uk

HarperCollins*Publishers*
Macken House, 39/40 Mayor Street Upper,
Dublin 1, D01 C9W8, Ireland

1

ISBN 978-0-00-856127-7

Adam Stower asserts the moral right to be identified
as the author and illustrator of the work.

A CIP catalogue record for this title is available from the British Library.

Printed and bound in the UK using 100% renewable electricity
at CPI Group (UK) Ltd

MIX
Paper | Supporting
responsible forestry
FSC™ C007454

This book contains FSC™ certified paper and other controlled
sources to ensure responsible forest management.

For more information visit: www.harpercollins.co.uk/green

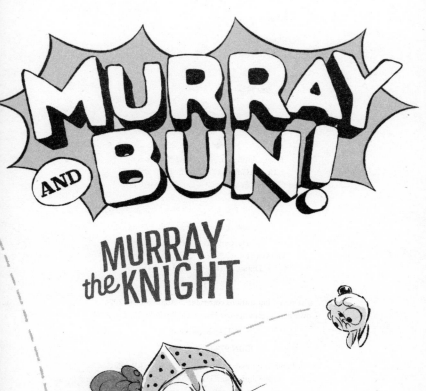

MURRAY AND BUN!

MURRAY the KNIGHT

ADAM STOWER

HARPERCOLLINS
CHILDREN'S BOOKS

In a little house in an ordinary town lives a wizard called Fumblethumb. Fumblethumb is a rubbish wizard. He is **terrible** at magic.

But this story isn't about Fumblethumb.

This story is about his cat, Murray, and the

magic cat flap.

This is Murray.

He likes things neat and tidy.

He likes snoozing, napping and sleeping (but not necessarily in that order).

He loves his bed and his fluffy blanket, Pickles.

He likes peace and quiet and warm sunshine (preferably dappled)

and dreams of one day having a custard-yellow cardigan of his very own.

He loves buns most of all, especially sticky ones with a cherry on top.

So you can imagine how he felt when Fumblethumb 'accidentally' turned his last and best bun into . . .

. . . a rabbit!

Meet Bun.

Bun is a very **bouncy** rabbit
with a cherry for a tail.

He is also quite sticky.

Bun loves EVERYTHING!

Especially adventure...

because it is **bound** to
be fun and lovely!

BUN!

Murray sleeps in a little bed by the back door of the kitchen where Fumblethumb works.

Every morning after elevenses, Murray steps through his cat flap to have a stretch in the garden, a wee, and a roll in the grass if he is feeling particularly sporty.

It was a good life.

... but **mostly**, it leads to ...

Adventure!!

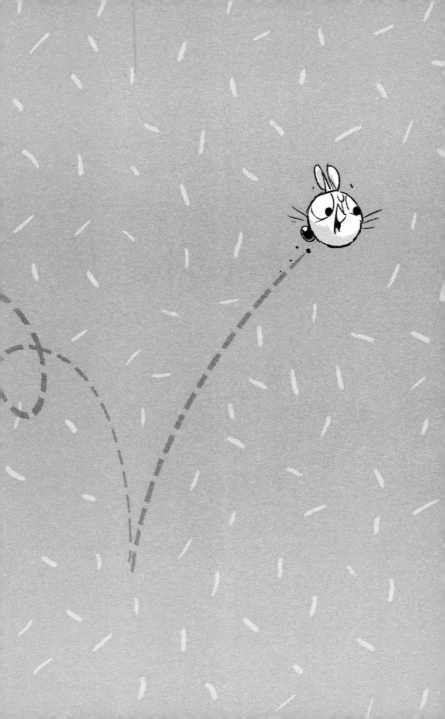

MURRAY the KNIGHT

Murray opened one eye.

Something was poking him. He rolled over
in his bed and blinked.

An ENORMOUS potato filled the little kitchen.

And it was getting bigger.

And BIGGER.

Murray sighed.
Fumblethumb was trying
magic *again*.

The MASSIVE spud shoved Murray across the floor and pressed him against the back door.

There was nothing for it. Murray picked up
Bun and slipped out through the cat flap . . .

He and Bun found themselves in a grand hall. An old king sat on a throne beside a princess.

She seems awfully cross, thought Murray. *How could anyone be so cross in such a marvellous hat?*

...um

'Well, I'm not marrying either of them, thank you very much,' huffed the princess.

'Really darling?' said the crumbly old king. He pointed at Murray. 'That one's a bit short and podgy, but he's delightfully furry.'

Murray blushed and poked his plump parts.

Bun, being a loyal rabbit, told Murray that he was beautiful just as he was.

Before Murray could say anything, a tall knight in black armour clanked forward and puffed out his polished chest.

'I am Sir Nasty! Defeater of Dragons, Slayer of Serpents, Masher of Monsters, Basher of Bandits and feared across the kingdom from the Silver Sea to the Bear Claw Mountains. The princess should be MINE!'

Bun piped up and said that that was all very well, but Murray was excellent at Tiddlywinks, could nap STANDING UP, looked fabulous in yellow and could hold THREE Custard Cream biscuits in his mouth at once without breaking them!

'Oh dear!' said the crumbly old king, looking from Murray to Sir Nasty and back again. 'What a pickle! How to choose, how to choose?'

'Simple!' boomed Sir Nasty. 'A contest! I challenge this portly fellow to a JOUST! The last man standing will marry Princess Rubytoes!'

'Like heck he
will!' muttered
the princess,
and she
promptly
climbed out of
the window . . .

. . . and ran off
across the gardens.

'Oh well!' said the king, watching Princess Rubytoes go. 'I suppose a joust it is.'

Sir Nasty grinned and swept past Murray and Bun.

'Um, the what?' asked Murray, who hadn't been listening. He had been thinking of the three Custard Cream biscuits that Bun had mentioned. His tummy was rumbling and Custard Cream biscuits were his third favourite thing*.

Bun filled Murray in on what he'd missed – and Murray admitted that he wasn't *absolutely* sure what jousting actually was.

Bun, being a happy-go-lucky rabbit, decided it probably involved trampolining, raspberry-flavoured cupcakes and funny hats.

*in his biscuit category.

Feeling much better, Murray bowed to
the king and left the throne room, with Bun
hopping after him.

They set off to find the jousting field.

The castle was enormous . . .

And somewhere . . .

. . . along the way . . .

. . . somehow . . .

. . . Bun vanished.

Bun was *always* going missing, grumbled
Murray.

He was such a curious rabbit.

And sticky.

Very sticky.

Suddenly, Murray spotted Bun outside, running through the castle gardens and disappearing among some tall hedges.

Murray hitched up his tights and chased after him, into the hedges. Bun shot along the pathways, turning this way and that.

And by the time
Murray caught up
with him . . .

. . . they were BOTH lost!

These weren't just any old hedges . . .

. . . This was a MAZE!

If they didn't find a way out soon, they were going to be late for the jousting. And Murray didn't want to be rude. He was a very polite cat and he always liked to be on time. And besides, he needed to find someone who would lend him a leotard, for all the trampolining.

Bun offered to help by bouncing really high and peeking over the hedgetops to find a way out.

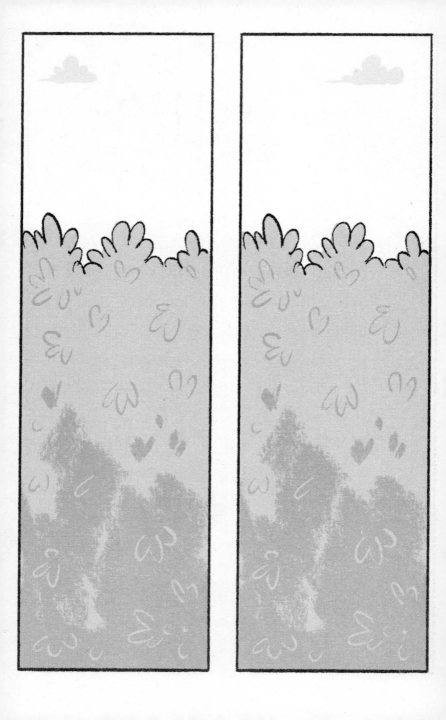

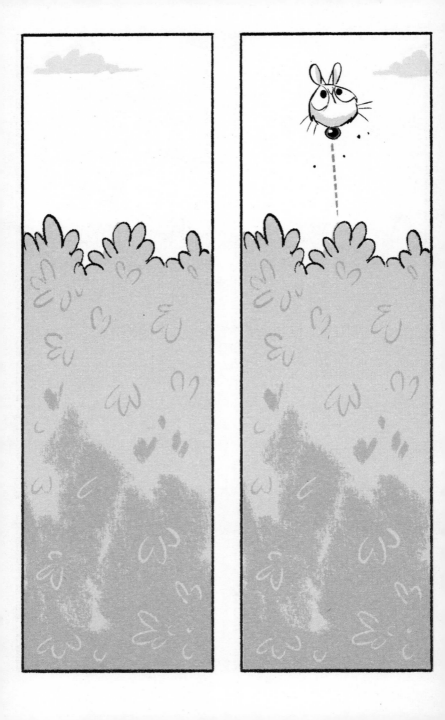

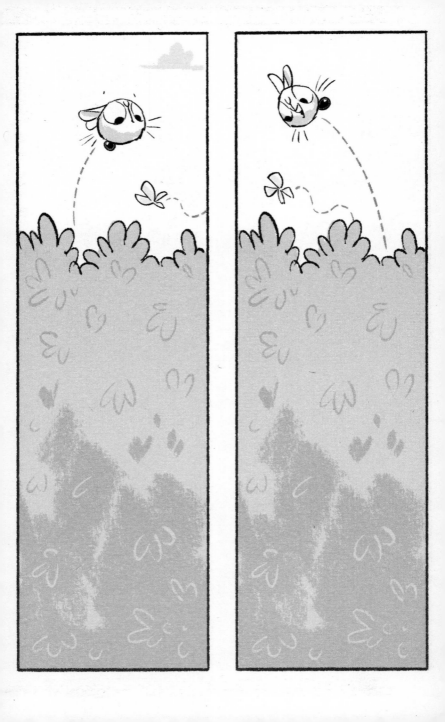

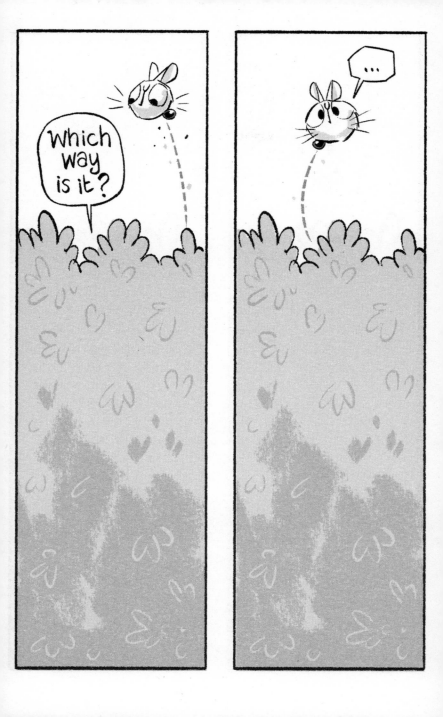

They had been lost long enough for Murray's tummy to start rumbling LOUDLY and for his legs to feel wobbly.

He was just thinking that what every maze should have is a bakery, when he heard a noise.

'Hold on, Bun! I can hear someone giggling! Follow me! Perhaps they know the way out!'

'AND they might have sandwiches,' he added hopefully. 'Herring ones!'

And when at last they reached the middle of the maze, they found, on a little bench . . . Princess Rubytoes!

She was stuck like glue to a muddy man in welly boots.

The man was probably just keeping his lips warm, thought Bun, testing the breeze with a wet finger.

But Murray's third cousin on his mother's side, Evangeline Petaldew, had been a poet's cat, so Murray knew all about these things . . .

He recognised LOVE when he saw it.

(But there were no sandwiches.)

When the princess spotted Murray, she jumped up with a squeak.

'Sir Murrray! Um, this is Muddy Mick,' she blushed. 'He's the gardener.'

Murray said hello, and Bun stuck himself to Mick's muddy face, just in case his lips were still a bit chilly.

Mmmmpf!

Princess Rubytoes looked worried. She sat Murray on the bench and took his paw in her hand.

'I love Muddy Mick,' she said. 'You won't tell, will you?'

'I love fresh air, digging, growing stuff, being outside and getting muddy. And Mick loves it too.'

"S'right,' nodded Mick, peeling Bun off his face. 'And the sound slugs make when ya poke 'em. Ain't that right, my love?'

'Oh yes, my darling. That too,' said Princess Rubytoes.

'You see, Sir Murray,' continued the princess, 'I'm fed up with stuffy castles, puffy dresses and pointy hats. So Mick has been teaching me all about gardening. And I love it!'

Princess Rubytoes sighed. 'Sir Nasty doesn't love me. He just wants to marry me so he can be king. Then he can sleep on piles of gold and order people around all day.'

'I think you're lovely,' said the princess to Murray. 'And your podgy bits are my favourite. But I love Mick, and . . . um . . . you are a *cat* after all, so it'd be a bit odd if we got married, wouldn't it?'

Murray was secretly relieved. He was very happy with Bun and his blanket, Pickles, thank you very much. And being a tidy cat, he wasn't a massive fan of mud, either.

He nodded nobly and told Princess Rubytoes that she should do whatever she wanted.

The princess grinned and gave Murray a big kiss on the cheek, which was very nice. But honestly, Murray would've preferred a big sandwich.

'Do you want to know a secret?' asked Princess Rubytoes, jumping to her feet.

Secrets often involved adventure, and so Murray was about to say, 'No, not really,' but . . . Bun had his own ideas.

Muddy Mick and the princess led Murray and Bun out of the maze . . .

. . . and through the castle gardens.

They came to a little door in a brick wall.

''ere we are,' said Mick, stepping through the door. 'This way.'

'You'll never believe your eyes,' said Princess Rubytoes, shoving Murray and Bun through the little door. 'It's Mick's secret garden . . .'

Murray's eyes bulged.

Bun did a triple somersault.

Growing all over Mick's garden were the BIGGEST vegetables they had EVER seen!

There were colossal cucumbers, tremendous turnips and super-sized spuds. Huge rhubarb creaked in the breeze and massive marrows covered the ground.

Murray and Bun had never seen such
VAST VEGETABLES!

Mick was a marvel!

Murray's favourite, and the biggest of the bunch, was an enormous parsnip, poking out of the ground.

'S'big'un, ain't it?' grinned Muddy Mick.

Murray looked from Mick to the princess.

'He says, "it's a big one, isn't it?"' Princess Rubytoes explained.

'Oh, yes!' nodded Murray. 'A whopper!'

'Bun!' added Bun.

Princess Rubytoes grinned.

'Keep this secret, but we've entered a competition. A BIG ONE! If we win FIRST PRIZE we can do whatever WE like. We'll have a massive garden all of our own and can grow the best veg in the whole kingdom!'

'We'll be so happy,' Princess Rubytoes added, hugging Mick tight enough to squeeze the puff out of him.

'The only thing that can stop us now is Sir Nasty,' said the princess.

'Tha's right!' said Mick.

He grabbed Murray by the shoulders. 'If Nasty wins the joust, he'll marry my Rubykins! I loves 'er, Sir Murray! I loves 'er more than sunrise. I loves 'er more than meat pies. The shine in 'er eyes gives me a tumble in my belly an' makes my legs turn to jelly!'

'You must win the joust, Sir Murray – you have to!' said Princess Rubytoes.

Murray smiled and patted Mick's hand. Murray loved raspberries, looked fabulous in funny hats, and was excellent on the trampoline. Sir Nasty didn't stand a chance!

To prove it, Murray fished about in his pocket, and showed Mick his medal.

'Trampolining?' said Mick.

'Best Bouncer?' gulped Princess Rubytoes.

Murray puffed out his chest. 'GRADE 1!'

'Oh,' said the princess, and she explained to Murray what jousting *really* was.

'No trampolining, then?' asked Murray, in a small voice, and he put his medal back in his pocket.

''fraid not,' said Mick. 'Jus' warhorses, sharp swords an' pointy lances.'

'Oh,' said Murray. Jousting didn't sound fun AT ALL. Far too adventurous.

Bun was SURE there were at least some pillows involved – and custard. Wasn't there?

'It's not for the faint-'earted,' said Mick.

Murray's heart suddenly felt VERY faint.

Bun stuck himself affectionately to Murray's head, but it didn't help.

And then Mick picked them both up and carried them to the jousting field.

It was time for the duel.

When they arrived at the field, Princess Rubytoes was taken to sit beside the king, and Mick returned to his garden to tend to his vegetables.

Murray and Bun were shown to a tent to get
ready.

Inside, some armour was laid out for Murray to try.

The first suit was too wide.

The next suit was too tall.

The last one will be just right, thought Murray. (He had read lots of fairy tales before.)

It wasn't. It pinched Murray's plump parts something rotten and the helmet kept slipping over his eyes, but it was the best of a bad bunch.

'Well, well, well! Don't you look terrific! I'm trembling in my boots!' boomed a voice.

Murray peeked out from under his helmet.

'I came by to check that you have everything you need for our joust,' said Sir Nasty. He twirled his moustache. 'I mean, we want it to be a fair contest, don't we, my portly fellow?' Murray nodded, but admitted that he didn't really know what he needed.

'Ah! Yes, well . . .' said Nasty, 'you'll need a sword, the sharper the better;

a shield, the bigger the better;

a war horse, of course,

and lastly, a long and pointy lance.'

'But,' he added, sucking air in through his teeth, 'I'm afraid I have terrible news. It's all my squire's fault, isn't it, Basil?' he said, grabbing his squire by the cloak.

'Eh?'

'Explain yourself to Sir Murray, you blithering nitwit!'

'Wait, what now?' said Basil.

'You left the armoury unlocked and all the swords were stolen, weren't they?' bellowed Sir Nasty.

'Then you sent the shields to the polishers, didn't you, knowing full well that today is joust day!'

'And if that wasn't bad enough, you had cabbage pie for breakfast and scared off all the horses with a parp on your bum-trumpet!'

'And how on earth you managed to set fire to a whole rack of lances while toasting crumpets, I'll never know!'

But, I didn't...

'ENOUGH!' shouted Sir Nasty. He bent Basil over and booted him out of the tent.

Sir Nasty turned to Murray.

'I can only apologise, my dear fellow,' he said with an oily grin. 'Do let me help. You can borrow some things of mine. We can't have you going out there empty-handed, can we?'

Murray shook his head. He felt worried. Even the mention of crumpets hadn't helped.

Sir Nasty rummaged in his bag and kitted Murray out with some 'special' things of his own.

First of all he gave Murray a sword and a shield.

Bun said that they looked a lot like an egg-whisk and a paper plate with a bit of string tied to the back, but Murray said that he was sure Sir Nasty knew what he was doing.

'I have a spare horse, too,' said Sir Nasty. 'He's a bit small and . . . er . . . *feathery*, but he has nerves of steel. He's called Colin.'

Colin did look a *bit* chicken-y, thought Murray, but it was very kind of Sir Nasty to share.

Bun asked if all horses had beaks.

Bun?

'All you need now is a lance,' said Sir Nasty. 'And I have just the thing. Here you go, take this. You're all set.'

'My, oh my!' Sir Nasty stood back to admire Murray. 'I think I ought to have kept all that special stuff for myself! But that's my problem, you see. I'm too lovely. Oh well. May the best man win! See you on the field! Haw, haw, haw!'

And with that, Sir Nasty left the tent.

'He seems nice,' said Murray.

Bun frowned. He squinted at Murray's lance. It reminded him of something.

It reminded him of . . .

'Sir Nasty pinched it, the rotten cheat! I'll never win first prize now,' cried Muddy Mick, and burst into tears.

Murray hated seeing a muddy man cry. He handed Bun his lance and went to Mick to comfort him.

'Don't worry, Mr Mick,' he said, 'I'll use something else.'

Chomp!

Murray patted Mick's hand and dabbed tears from his muddy face with the tip of his hanky.

Chomp!
Chomp!
Chomp!

Soon, Muddy Mick stopped sobbing.

'Thanks, Sir Murray,' he sniffed.

Chomp! Chomp! Chomp! Chomp!

Murray had a nagging feeling that he shouldn't have left Bun with the giant parsnip after all.

Mick burst into tears. Again.

BONG!

A bell *bonged*. And somewhere outside, a bunch of trumpets blew a fanfare.

TARAAAAA-TARA
TARRRAAAAAA!

It was time for the duel.

Without a lance, Murray felt more wobbly than ever.

Bun felt bad about the parsnip, so he quickly made Murray an EXTRA JAMMY jam sandwich to settle his nerves. It usually worked a treat, but . . .

There was a terrible accident . . .

. . . and this time the jam just made things worse.

But there was no time to do anything about it now.

With a squelch, Murray sat on Colin.

He grabbed his sword and shield.

Mick stepped up, dipped his hand into his pocket and handed Murray a tear-stained carrot for a lance.

'It's no massive parsnip,' he said, 'but it's all I got.'

Time was up.

Outside, a crowd of villagers lined the field, jostling in their seats to get a better view.

The king and Princess Rubytoes were there too, sitting on their thrones.

The king hushed the crowd.

'Welcome!' he wheezed. 'Is everyone ready? Then let the joust . . . BEGIN!'

The trumpets TA-RAAA-ed again and the crowd wriggled with excitement.

Sir Nasty was the first to appear. He rode out of his tent on his mighty war horse ThunderClops. He twirled his moustache and ThunderClops snorted and pawed the ground.

'OOOOOOOOOOOOH!' oooh-ed the crowd.

Next came Sir Murray.
He trotted out of his
tent on Colin.

Colin took one look at Sir
Nasty, squawked, and laid
three eggs on the spot.

Then *she* flapped out from
under Murray and ran back
into the tent to hide.

'Oh . . .' oh-ed the crowd.

'Haw-haw-haw!' chuckled Sir Nasty.

'THUNDERCLOPS!
CHAAAAAARGE!' he
cried, and he set off at full
speed towards Murray.

Being a sensible cat, and very protective of his plump parts, Murray turned to run as fast as his paws could manage to join Colin under the bed in the tent.

But . . . his legs . . . didn't . . . budge!

'What courage!' gasped the crowd.

'How fearless!' sighed Princess Rubytoes.

'Um, no,' said Murray, 'it's the jam! It's oozed into my armour. It's gummed up my joints! Can we stop, please?' he asked, as politely as he could manage – but no one could hear him!

Sir Nasty couldn't believe his eyes! The little fur-bag hadn't even flinched!

'I'm the fearless one around here!' said Sir Nasty, drawing his sword and swishing it heroically through the air.

Murray strained to raise his shield and waggle his whisk . . . but . . . his arms didn't move either!

'What bravery!' cheered the crowd. Two milk maids and Big Bill the Butcher swooned with the excitement of it all.

'Muh - ray! Muh - ray!' chanted the king, who had never before seen such daring!

'My HERO!' whooped Princess Rubytoes.

By now, Sir Nasty was FUMING!

'If ANYONE is going to be the hero, it's going to be ME!' he boomed, aiming his lance and charging at Murray faster than ever.

The ground shook and Murray's plump parts jiggled as ThunderClops zoomed across the ARENA OF CERTAIN DEATH! Murray closed his eyes and wished he was back home with his blanket Pickles and a plate of foreign cheeses . . .

ThunderClops came closer and closer, and the tip of Sir Nasty's pointy lance came whizzing through the air . . .

nearer and nearer . . .

. . . right up . . .

. . . until the moment when . . .

. . .ThunderClops saw . . .

. . . the carrot!

AAAAAA

. . . stop!

'WHAAAAAAAAAAAAAAAAAAAAAA!'
screamed Sir Nasty, as he was thrown from his
saddle to soar through the air . . .

. . . and landed . . .

. . . in the water trough.

Luckily for Murray, carrots were ThunderClops' second-favourite* crunchy treat.

(*in his root vegetable category, after parsnips.)

Murray breathed a sigh of relief and was hoping that a kind passer-by might scratch his itchy nose for him, when he saw something that made him gulp.

It was Sir Nasty!

...nom nom nom...

He had clambered out of the trough and was dripping wet and FURIOUS! Steam hissed from his ears as he raised his sword.

'Now you're for the CHOP, you infuriating fur ball!' he boomed, as he lunged towards Murray.

Murray stood helpless, glued to the spot. The crowd held their breath.

But with every step . . .

. . . Sir Nasty . . .

slowed . . . down . . .

. . . until . . . just inches . . .

from Murray . . .

. . . he shuddered . . .

to a standstill.

'ARRRGH!

I'M ALL RUSTED UP!' he cried.

And with that, Sir Nasty wobbled this way and that, toppled over, and fell to the ground with a loud CLANK!

Murray had WON!

The crowd went WILD!

Bun carried Murray off the field and propped him up inside their tent.

The crowd followed the king and Princess Rubytoes and Muddy Mick as they all rushed over to see Murray.

'Brave Sir Murray! What a champion!' said the king. 'Well, you gave Nasty a thrashing, that's for sure! Whatever you want, it's yours!'

'I want . . .' said Murray thoughtfully. He wriggled in his armour. 'I want . . .'

The crowd held their breath. Again.

'A tin opener, please.'

The crowd deflated.

'And he wants me to be a gardener with Muddy Mick!' interrupted Princess Rubytoes, hopping up and down on the spot. 'Don't you, Sir Murray?'

The king looked at Murray and raised a bushy eyebrow. 'Really?'

'Oh yes, sorry, that too,' Murray nodded. 'And the tin opener.'

The crowd burst into cheers and hip-hip-hoorays. The princess squeaked with happiness. 'EEEEEK! Thank you, Sir Murray! You are my HERO!'

She gave him another big kiss, picked up Muddy Mick and ran out of the tent . . .

. . . and CRASHED straight into a little man.

They helped the man up and dusted him down.

'Hold on,' he said, adjusting his glasses. 'Are you Muddy Mick?'

'Arr,' nodded Mick.

'The gardener?' asked the little man.

'That's right,' said Princess Rubytoes.

'Marvellous!' The little man grinned.

'Congratulations! This is for you.'

He snapped his fingers and two large men stepped forwards, carrying a glittering trophy and an enormous chest of gold coins.

Muddy Mick and Princess Rubytoes had WON
the First Prize in the gardening competition!

It was very exciting! Murray would have hopped up and down if he could. Bun made up for it by doing NINE somersaults.

'Well, well! It looks like we're having a party,' chuckled the king. 'But first, I'll get you that tin opener,' he added, patting his belly and winking. 'In my chubbier days I used to get wedged in my armour too! It played havoc with my plump parts.'

'But when you're done, bring it with you up to the castle,' added the king. 'We will need it for the FEAST!'

'Feast?' asked Murray.

'Oh, yes! To celebrate. You can't have a party without a FEAST! We'll need the tin opener for all the JUMBO cans of HERRING TRIFLE. It's Princess Rubytoes' second favourite.*'

(*in her canned food category.)

'*Herring Trifle!*' swooned Murray.

Bun got Murray's jammy armour
off in record time . . .

. . . and they were up to the castle and across the drawbridge in a jiffy.

Murray loosened his belt,

picked up Bun and stepped through the gate . . .

. . . and back into the little kitchen on Collywobble Close.

'Hello, you two!' said Fumblethumb, from somewhere behind the MASSIVE potato. 'Looks like spuds for tea, OK?'

Murray sighed. He climbed under Pickles
to dream of Herring Trifle.
Tomorrow was another day.
Luckily for Bun, he *loved* spuds.

THE END

For Murray